GOGGLES!

EZRA JACK KEATS

For Fran Manushkin

Collier Books
Macmillan Publishing Company
New York

Macmillan Publishing Company, 866 Third Avenue, New York, NY 10022. Collier Macmillan Canada, Inc.
Library of Congress catalog card number: 70-78081. Printed in the United States of America.
First Collier Books Edition 1971. ISBN 0-02-044100-2
8 9 10 11 12 13 14 15 16 17

"Archie, look what I found,"
Peter shouted through the pipe.
"Motorcycle goggles!"
Archie watched Peter through the hole.
He listened and smiled.

Peter ran to the hideout
and put on the goggles.
"Aren't they great?" he asked.
Archie smiled and nodded.

Peter said, "Let's go over
to your house and sit on the steps."
Archie nodded.

They started off.
Suddenly some big boys appeared.
"Give us those goggles, kid!"
"No, they're mine," Peter said.
His dog Willie growled.
"Archie, hold Willie," said Peter.

Peter stuffed the goggles into his pocket
and put up his fists.
Archie gasped.
Peter turned to see if something was wrong.

The next thing he knew
he was knocked to the ground.
Everyone stared at the goggles.

Before anyone could move, Willie snatched
the goggles and ran through a hole in the fence.
The big boys chased after him.
"Meet you at the hideout," whispered Peter.
"You go this way, I'll go that way.
They won't know where we're going.
Willie will find us!"

Peter raced to the hideout.

He sank down as low as he could.

Footsteps!

"The big boys! They followed me."

Peter held his breath.

ARCHIE!

What was that?

Archie looked through the hole.

There were the big boys—
and there was Willie.
They would see him!

Archie stared at the pipe.
Suddenly he spoke.
"Here, Willie, through the pipe—fast!"

WILLIE!

Peter peeked through the hole.
The big boys were coming—
closer and closer.

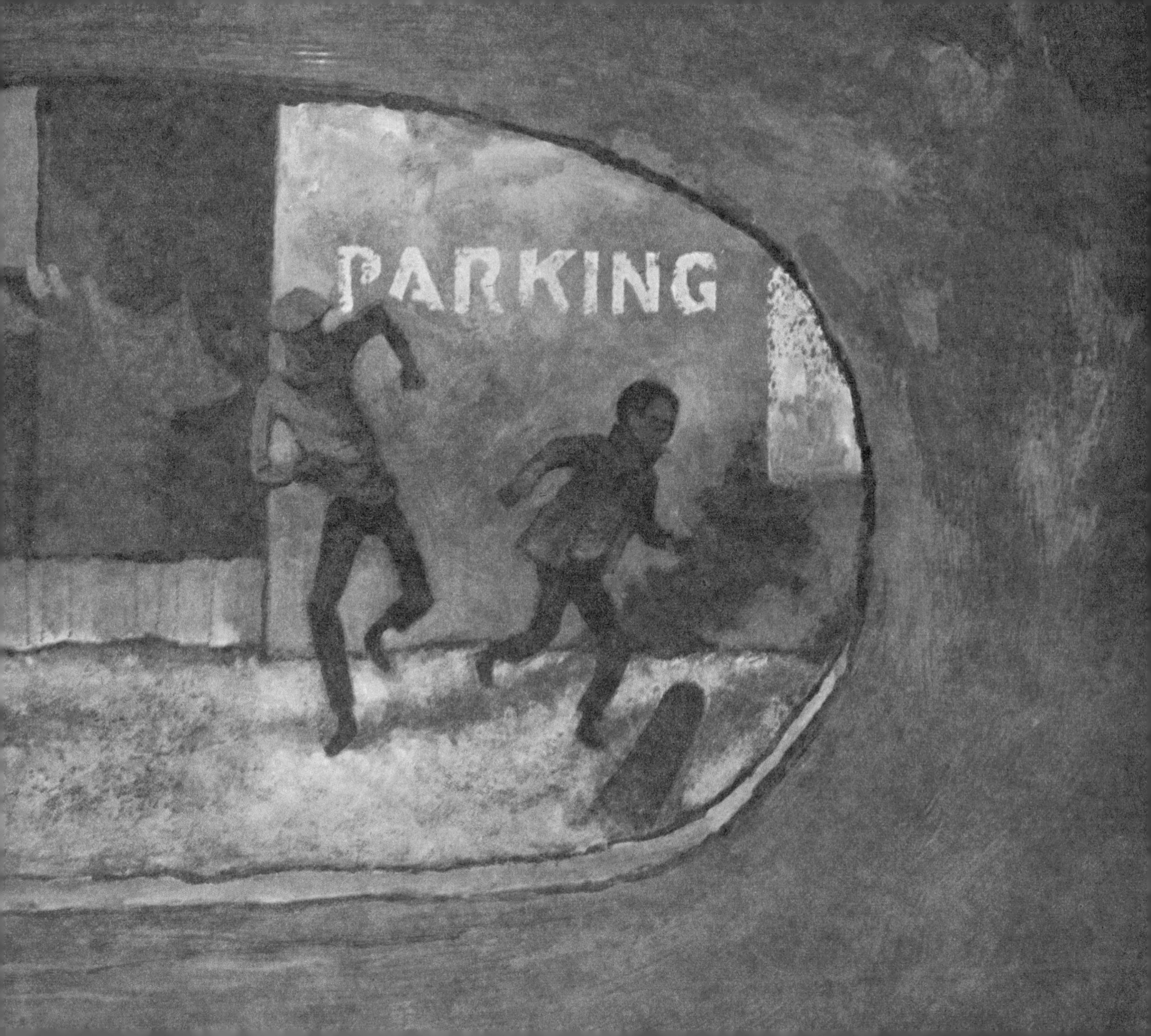
PARKING

Peter took a deep breath.
Then he yelled through the pipe,
"Willie—meet us at the parking lot!"
"Head for the parking lot!" one of the big boys yelled.
"Let's go!"

Peter, Archie and Willie crept out of the hideout.
When they reached the fence they got up and ran.

They got to Archie's house.
Archie laughed and said,
"We sure fooled 'em, didn't we?"
"We sure did," said Peter,
handing him the goggles.
"Things look real fine now," Archie said.
"They sure do," said Peter.